Elena Guro

THE
LITTLE CAMELS
OF
THE SKY

Translated by Kevin O'Brien

Ardis

Copyright ©1983 by Ardis

No part of this publication may be reproduced
in any manner without the written permission
of the publisher.

Ardis Publishers
2901 Heatherway
Ann Arbor, Michigan 48104

Library of Congress Cataloging in Publication Data

Guro, Elena, 1877-1913.
    The little camels of the sky.

    I. Title.
PG3467.G9L5   1982   891.71'3   82-16380
ISBN 0-88233-437-9 (cloth)
ISBN 0-88233-438-7 (pbk.)

CONTENTS

ACKNOWLEDGEMENTS

This translation is for Idee Brown, who best understood Guro's spirit.

I would like to thank Professor Simon Karlinsky for his patience and dedication in going over the text, and for his many corrections and suggestions.

And I would also like to thank Professor Vladimir Markov for his explication of numerous "thorny" passages in the work.

—Kevin O' Brien

I want to worship youth alone, youth alone.

Speak of the storm, so children won't grow up knowing nothing of the storm. . .

AN AD IN THE PAPER
Extra Warm Undershirts, Drawers, Socks, Tummywarmers
Made from Camel Down

Here's how it happens: they ambush shining young spirits, tall and kindly, looking like golden, lanky little camels covered with down of a sacred sheen.

Cracking whips in the air, they herd them into a bunch. The tender good-natured creatures—too good to understand how others cause pain—crowd and huddle together, stretch their necks across one another, press against the coarse enclosure, and lose their tender down in that crush.

Then they gather this down of the little camels of the sky (which is specially warm with a life-giving spring warmth) from off the ground and weave undershirts from it.

"You mean they just kill those poor little camels?" I was asked anxiouxly.

"Why kill them?" They drive them and drive them till enough of their down rubs off and then release them back to the sky till the next time. And in a mere minute their down grows back even better than before.

The distant, unbearably pure strips northered.

All day, amid clouds, lakes swam like swans, proud in the azure. A thawed patch of rosy sky lived among the black birches—and breathed.

Breathed. And the birches were wet.

From upper air heralds headed past patches of thawed sky, past all the sloping sky.

And they were heard only by the tender and proud souls of trees lit from the depths of the horizons, and by towers not understood by anyone,

and by the tender tumbled sky, pressing its caressing palms to the earth.

And they went along the sky—which had neared the earth and grown submissive in its sereneness—along the straw-toned and tender sky which no longer shunned the earth. And tiny twigs stirred in that sky, troubled and touched by the city's nearness. The twigs watched tram after tram fly past.

Heralds passed—and the illumined souls of the remote summits and towers heard them.

And those already revealed heard—and prayed.

And somewhere lay lakes...lakes...lakes.

When a young man goes to meet the north, the wind beats his brow, his high pure brow, not yet knowing fear.

Hair streaming like a horse's forelock. And horse-like mettle toward what's ahead—while ahead lie...lakes...lakes.

Somewhere a little porch was thawing then, and a larch stretched, fir-like, over it. And the larch breathed.

YOU CAN'T SHOW THIS TO EVERYONE, CAN YOU?

Forgive me singing about you, shoreline;
    You're so proud.
Forgive my suffering for you—
    When people, not noticing your beauty,
Violate you and chop your forest.
    You're so distant
And inaccessible.
    Your soul disappears like the luster
Of the bay
    When you see it close at your feet.
Forgive my coming and upsetting
    The purity of your solitude,
Of your reign.

*

*   *

Like a mother muffling her son's throat with a scarf, I followed the soaring of your ships, proud proud creatures of spring!

We don't want to indulge but to overcome ourselves. Workers would buy sunflower seeds—let's buy some—why are we any better? Our squeamishness is sad and it binds us.

Mr. poet! You're dropping your notebook overboard!

The yacht soared on the sea. We suddenly saw a black belly in that sea... just lying there... And we tacked so skillfully that the boat became winged like a slice of salmon... And played among the waves... it couldn't get enough of it— again and again!

And the waves were impressive.

Are we going to end our friendship?.. Not likely—after all, we're travelers together—the storm's behind us, spring ahead!..

We were swung and tossed up.

Separation is only for those who hang back like cowards... O, to fly somewhere together and leap and choke down shining spray...

All together... right now!..

The wind blew toward us and the larches smelled lovely.

At the exhibition of our friends, the public roared with laughter. Great! Great!.. Will your little drama end soon?.. We have faith on credit! We have faith...

Yesterday we barely made it back from the sea coast... the waves lashed, the wind whined like a mosquito in my hair—death! death!.. Great! Great! The public roared with laughter.

And the larches shone with spring.

[16]

How funny the little camel was! He prepared diligently for his exams, and then flunked out because of shyness and eccentricity. And at dawn, instead of poking his nose in his pillow, he wrote poems on the sly.

Being diligent, he deprived himself of the joy of the spring sky's first leaves. Still, he couldn't manage to keep his pants from sliding above his belt or his shirt from bunching up... or to act right before strangers.

He couldn't play tennis, and couldn't pretend he simply didn't want to. And everyone saw that he couldn't because of shyness... and that he wanted to hide his shyness and couldn't do that either. With anguish, he realized they could tell, even when his back was turned, how unbearably awkward he felt... So he usually saw fun as something moving off or flashing in the distance through trees.

Yes, but the cranes' untouched dawns shine at the bottom of mirror-like lakes. Lonely pure skies.

As the littl camel looked at the sky, in that rosy sky a warm kindred region brimmed over.

The crowned fir keeps rushing up into the blue abyss, keeps remaining before my eyes, yet keeps rushing up in victory.

Then I'm filled with great shame for all my "costs and damages." We promise not to lower our eyes when those we love meet us with mockery. (And those in whom we believed yesterday—or just this morning.) No! We'll take their mockery into our quiet, bright, wide-open eyes and bear it like a badge on our breast... not hiding it.

This is the mockery of one to whom I wish happiness.

May all my daydreams gather round your head—the daydreams of a happy dreamer—round you, my sad sad mocker.

*

* *

I'm dumb, I'm untalented, I'm clumsy, but I pray to you tall firs. I'm really awfully clumsy, I'm... a coward. Yesterday I became frightened of a man I don't respect. It's from cowardice that I don't know how to ride a bicycle. I haven't got a drop of will power, but I pray to you tall firs.

Yesterday I just couldn't get myself to tell a kind lady who gave me milk and cookies that I—write decadent verses, from the agonizing fear that she might ask where I'm published. No, I said that my chief mission in life was to teach enthusiastically. Today I'm kicking myself with shame and repentence.

Yesterday I finished some poems not at all the way I'd wanted, anyhow I knew they'd laugh at me. But now that they've all gone to the train station for some open-air festivity—I pray to you tall firs, without you I'm very dumb, very...

Over there stand tsars crowned with candles...

In the free, free upper air, above the crown of tsars, an empty flagpole bores tenderly into the blue.

I make a vow here: never to be ashamed of my real self ("real"—that self which writes poems they don't want to print anywhere).

Not to be nervous when entering a drawing room, and no matter how many unpleasant guests are there—not to forget that I'm a poet, not a worm...

And never to desire to be printed in their magazines, to be like all the rest, or to take the lives of animals. Why do I think that also?

The poet is the giver, but not the taker of life... Look how nice the world is—washed clean by the sun, it already believes in your feeling and your future writings, and looks at you with gratitude...

The poet is the giver of life, but not an aggressor, the taker. And I promise to make no bones about telling elegant hunters—no matter how attractive they are—that they're villains, villains!

And so what if no one cares for me—I'm strong!

But will I keep my word?.. Will I keep it?

I clench my fists, but I'm alone, and around me—such majesty.

All this leaves me so quickly.......

My hand lifted a stone and hurled it... spiraling, it traced an arc above the edge of the forest, in the blue land... All its life it was on earth, and suddenly my hand gave it flight... Did it feel bliss, flying through the blue?

*

*   *

Green curls flutter in the sky.
The sky laughs.
Flags at dachas dash,
flow from proud flagpoles,
splash in the blue wind.

*

*   *

Scatterbrain, madman, soarer,
maker of spring storms,
sculptor of restless thoughts,
driving the azure!
Listen you mad seeker,
rush, dash,
shoot past, unshackled
intoxicator of storms.

*

   *   *

Dreamers, swear here someday,
seeing the upsweep,
seeing the upsweep of tall firs,
the soaring of distant ships,
seeing sharp summits sway in the sky,
entrusting to no one their proud purity—
Swear to a dream and unfading faithfulness,
proud knighthood of madness!
And be faithful to your youth
And the plight of sky.

*

   *   *

Earth, tell me why one soul will fall silent in youth,
while another soul sings, sings of you...

Sings of you with immeasurable voice.
And sings, earth, of your kind sun!

How is it that one soul lives, is lovely, and then suddenly falls silent and lives without a voice, as though there were nothing more for it to say its entire life?..

A PACT

If you want to ally yourself with that which makes the piny depths mysterious and the pale sky divine; if you're filled with the firmness of ancient sagas, and when you had read them a northern pride awoke in you, and a longing to stomp your feet and toss your head high (with its unplaited mane)—run straight before you to the sky's bright brink.

"Stomp, stomp—a round meadow!"

"Who are you?" unseen ones shout, so it whistles in your ears.

You answer:

"A conqueror!"

"Insolent!"

"I'm a creator. I'm Balder's bright hurricane!"

And your stomping can be heard.

Ahead—amid gaps in the tips of firs—the molten velvet of sunset. Its voice is silence. It's a sign, addressed to you—and already implying a pact. Put your fingers to your lips! Shsh!..

At twilight you return, feeling neither your feet nor the road. You, a human, have turned into a twilight creature. You're full of understanding, but don't feel like talking. You could speak with deep quiet signs—the way the evening's quiet sky speaks. It's already completely dark in the house... only some windows staring into the room... You undress without a candle—in deference to the sensitive guardians of the night.

But if you are unfaithful and inflexible; if you rush to rid yourself of that which makes you special and is uniquely yours... If the lonely hours of the eve of sacrifice frighten you—and the feat of pure silence, and the bitter offenses of those who seem to you splendid—then you must fear the white nights and the long twilights of summer's beginning, and these guardians of twilight when the signs are wrought.

But will my being marked as special stop altogether?

You'll tell a friend: "In some ways, I don't love the white nights! They weary me... they watch me... and I feel lost. I don't love them though they're lovely!"

Because, human, you betrayed your dreams one day. You surrendered. Forgot what went before... you didn't even notice that. You said: "My youth's past—I'm already over thirty... we all calm down."

But from that time the white nights began to torment you. Walking in the garden you're ashamed to weep, to pray before a jasmine bush or birch trunk in the white nights. You no longer go out several times each evening (always with that same stirring) to meet a whitening trunk or spire, the tower of a pine tip at the end of a path... And you're right to fear! Better try to arrange it so you won't meet those eyes, those summons... in the white nights! In the white nights!

But evenings of the young summer can be as bright and transparent as tears!

I was returning to the city from visiting where it had been very bright, festive and painful. Because there are certain imposing rooms—blinding and filled with a loud, unconstrained, detached din that's complete without you. Rooms always painful and awkward to enter, in which you always wind up a pauper or a fool, and from which you depart into the darkness, feeling like an orphan in this wide world. Such rooms before Christmas—that greedy feastday of the fortunate—are simply unbearable.

You glance back at the radiant windows once more—no, nowhere, never yet, were lights in windows so beautiful. Or did people live so glitteringly and gaily!..

Towards evening it was quiet and pleasant when I wearied of waiting for my train on the little forest platform. Through the darkness one sensed many, many trees at hand, and something important was happening in that darkness.

The earth had thawed, roofs dripped; and in the lamplight impetuous wet twigs prayed with shy rapture into the close, trusting, warm sky.

A semiphore was glancing at me with its friendly green eye. I paced up and down the short wooden platform, and kept watching the twigs (which gleamed with water beads beneath the dim, solitary light) pray into the deep, quiet sky.

This lasted a long time, and my soul began to hear more than usual, and I heard the earth ask it:

"Listen, you're so near me now, you hear the voices of the air and of snow-drip... you can also hear me. You see, I have some worries. I have certain children I must entrust to someone. Search for, shelter my children—they're very clumsy and silent... instead of speaking loudly, proudly, they scarcely move their lips.

Defend my children—others have offended them. They

work in offices instead of writing poems... instead of enjoying me in freedom.

Most important—no one notices that they're beautiful because their shoe laces hang loose; their breeches are stretched over their little knees; and freckles sit all awry on their noses—yes, on their noses and above their eyes. They don't know how to bow without backing away and stepping on surrounding shoes!

Accept my children—they're shy. When one should remain silent, in their fright they speak frightfully loud, so that everyone looks round in indignation. But back at their hovels they toss on their beds in anguish... recalling their feats among polite society—it's so unbearably embarrassing they're ready to scream and bite from bashfulness. But no one understands that, what it means to fall into a frenzy and bite from bashfulness.

Though I weep over them, I can do nothing for them: switches and canes are torn from me to beat my children.

She spoke in kindly grief and rays ran from her... caressing, mild and moist like down; and the thaw and birches prayed, just as someone young feels both pity and fear toward someone stern near him.

The smell of melted snow swept over me. Whistles whirled from behind the bend. A locomotive leapt, eyes flashing.

The forest station stayed behind me, dripping tender voices, and now it was as though I bore a treasure in my breast or went to stand sentry somewhere.

From beyond the forest, the shrill whistles seemed resin-fresh and fearless.

*

*   *

Pine boughs bending: a flame.
Golden signs stand above the dune, in the evening sky.

They deceived you, your elders. Year after year they deceive the young. But I'm a mother, I can't be bought, I'll tell the truth.

Yes, they deceived you—they taught you to say, "One's future lies in a secure job..." A young man can't risk his whole future... It's too serious. After all, his whole life's ahead!..

But they can't deceive me, a mother, when eyes which I gazed on like the sky grow dim from copying meaningless papers.

Tell me, you twelve-year-old boy—what do you imagine when they say "the future" to you? A field, a meadow, the sun, a stream and a boat... right? Not a pile of paper or a cardtable in some smoke-filled club, every night till dawn...

Well listen! They won't give you your future! They're deceiving you—they won't give you that meadow, boat, stream! With those faded eyes, you won't find your future now—those friends, that girl, that path which promised you your real happiness! Your eyes are faded, after all! Spring no longer weaves soft shadows over your eyebrows. Light no longer streams from your half-lowered, bashful face...

"What a fine young man your Vasya's become!"

O, yes, they've forced you to acquire the official bearing —when entering a room you no longer shrink, shrug your shoulders and hunch your neck, tender little camel!

It's a lie. None of you think about young men, you care only about old men like yourselves and that you understand.

You hate youth, you envy it too much—you persecute it and cut it to your measure so it won't sting you with its purity, integrity and capacity for real creativity.

When you lisped on about a "secure job," you were thinking of an old man with a bald spot and pot belly, travelling to Karlsbad.

And this young man—you forced him when still a boy to spend all his spring months in the city, gazing in sad boredom day after day at the gray stone courtyard of the prep school, with the hopeless dull gaze of those who've submitted to penal servitude.

Year after year you deprived him of spring! —Of little violet stars in the spring forest, of yellow butterflies in the morning—of merry daisies like little suns in a sea of grassy juice. When he wouldn't submit, you forced him, not sparing any means—and if you didn't beat him, worse—you deceived him: "Study, Vasya, study, you'll become smarter!.."

O, did you seriously believe he'd grow smarter, deprived in those most sensitive years of all God's earth? Study from the cradle! What about spring? Are you supposed to learn to love spring when you've grown coarse, worn out?

Smarter! But didn't you yourself say, "What good are all these textbooks, so stupidly written—in any case it'll just be forgotten, and it's completely useless!"

While you provided yourself with poets' works, music, flowers, dachas, trips abroad?!

"And what about Vasya?" Vasya's got to study! You've hated your Vasya, you've envied his youth, you hurried to squeeze him into a uniform with epaulettes, so he wouldn't sting you: with his bright young body reminding you of an angel and a heaven you'd forgotten. "Smoothe down those cowlicks!—you look so inspired!" you remarked ironically when suddenly you saw, through your regimentation, that a sun had burst forth in him.

You sent him off to military school, made him take each step to the crackling of a drum and the shouts of drill. While each year at that time the birdcherry bloomed and scattered its blossoms, and swallows wove their nests!

People sometimes gaze at greenery with the most frenzied greed! Don't you know that? Have you forgotten? You've forgotten for good, you no longer know.

You tore him away from his little animals, the only creatures that understood him.

And did you ever ask him then what he himself desired, what he longed for?

Huggin the dog's neck, he resisted and cried on that hazy morning when you sent him off to military school. You did that for his happiness? For the happiness of awkward, lanky Vasya, as he was then? Yes?.. No! You simply killed that Vasya, sacrificing him to the future bald gentleman with hemorrhoids who was then born into the world from the corpse of the youth you had tormented. A bald gentleman, resembling you—who've lost the very taste and meaning of life...

You deceived me, his mother, on that morning as well. You forced me to be a hypocrite and plead. "Papa's so upset I have an aneuryism. Vasya, you've got to spare Mama." And on that morning we killed my Vasya. No, worse—we lured him into a trap, tossed him into a wolf pit where for years he lay rotting with his broken legs—where his soul lay dying of hunger—for years—then it died. And like two accomplices we went away from the pit, ignoring his cries for help.

And at night, how much he wept there... alone, biting his pillow. —He was happy then?

Later, an adult, he'll come to me and say: "I've met her, I sense that it's she! Why didn't she recognize me? Mama, why can't it ever be mutual?"

What can I tell him?

Your girl? She'll fall in love with my Vasya! Vasya with his shy face and trusting eyes and his rakelike hands dangling awkwardly... But they've "given you bearing" my darling, and I myself hardly recognize you! You've acquired bearing and become quite a young man! You, my confidential clerk! Love, that Girl, the Sun, the meadow, the stream. No, forget all that now, just find yourself a solid match now!

Comrades, friends! Why?! You can find colleagues anywhere, anytime. Why this mission of yours? You'll get your
periodic rewards, career advances. My darling, that's no
meadow spread before you, but the civil service or a commer-
cial career—just as we had hoped for you.

Well then, you're probably happy now?

Where's your smile?

They made a fire on its roots and burnt the heart of a living pine.

Who? I don't know.

The tree with its heavy curly head (immense with life strength) was held up by a third of its fiber, though freakishly deprived of its proud support and balance.

There was a deep quiet. Doomed to a slow death, the tree kept silent. Without doubt it knew what they had done to it—and its companions kept silent. And it was unpleasant, painful to see the expression of its head, its mighty boughs— just as it's painful to see a very healthy person in the midst of life who's been released for a time, after which he's irrevocably condemned to hang, and he himself knows this, and those around him... and everyone keeps silent.

I went back through the felled area.

Do you feel spite, forest, when your treetops—used to strolling in the sky, to hearing legends told by constellations, to lullabying the clouds—fall against the earth, desecrated by man? No, you've grown beyond the possibility of spite. I too have grown beyond spite... but I feel so blue.

*

*   *

When already bedridden, he kept repeating: "No, I know I'm not a knight, I'm simply Alonza the Good!" And he asked their forgiveness that he'd troubled them with his madness. They comforted him and cheered him, deliberately calling him "Knight!"

They gave him that like a rattle, now when he was already bedridden and dying. "Well, let the poor fellow finally play with his dream!"

"No, I'm not a knight. You've brought me to reason. I know, you see, I'm no longer that proud madman—I'm simply Alonzo the Good."

—Mama, was Don Quixote kind?

—He was.

—But they beat him... I'm sorry for him. Why did they?

—So there'd be adventures, so it'd be funny to read.

—Poor man, it hurt him, and he was kind. I'm sorry he's already dead.   Did he die a long time ago?

—Oh stop it now, what does it matter? It's make-believe, Lyolya. There never was a Don Quixote.

—But why'd they write a book then? Mama, you mean they lie in books?

—You're interrupting my sewing, get to bed.

—If a book lies, it must be an evil book. They're bad to Don Quixote in it... But he came to life. He came to me yesterday... sat on my bed and sighed and went away... He was so tall, and barely stumbled along...

—Lyolya, look out or I'll punish you. I won't put up with senseless chatter.

*

   *   *

Rain fell, it was cold. Near the station a man stood in the darkness... and got drenched. In grief he forgot to go under the roof. He didn't notice that he was soaked and chilled. He even stood, unsuspecting, right under the gutter...

He didn't notice that he was chilled and kept standing like a stupified homeless bird, getting drenched. Water washed onto him from above, laughing and dancing in a thick stream.

About three days later he died.

That was my son, my son... my unhappy only child.

That wasn't my son at all, I'd never seen him. But I loved him because he got drenched like a homeless bird, and in his deep grief didn't notice it.

*

   *   *

And so tender and merciful was that evening with its high, pensive brow that indeed it deserved to be punished for its mercy and compassion and love. Punished with pain for its purity and height.

And it also had a right to be crucified—that tender evening looking like spring, and the distant forgotten homeland of the soul.

Е. Гуро.

And now rain rays onto the poet's body!

Hotter! —Onto the translucent fingers where the noble bones of Sir Marquis of the Clouds show through.

Burn brighter! —Bring back their rosy color!

See how unwillingly the weak sinews have joined the long neck to the shoulders.

Be generous to him—he's lost much, the mad scatterbrain! —And see, the bones are translucent, like bright knots beneath his patient skin—and on his high temples there's blue sky.

Scorch him well! —Serves him right!

He's laughing? —What?! Life returns to you, prodigal, squanderer, funny little camel?!

You're pleased, aren't you?..

At the dune horses snort nervously, stretching their muzzles and spreading their tails—while spirits in bright garments pass near and melt away. They pass and vanish this instant, like white vapor.

It's hot!

"No, after all, I can't do without dreams: I bear within me the golden blue body of something young, and when I drink life in, it drinks also—such are poets. What's to be done?"

"Be economical."

"That's just what I'll do."

JUNE

Deep, deep the blue.
The forest's full of heat.
Needles hang, rapt...
and ring faintly in sleep.

Deep, deep the needles.
Full of heat
and happiness.
Rapt with rapture.

But, you know, you're bluer than the sky, dragonfly. "I'm a princess!" The sky's deep blue. The thick ringing of a bee has arisen, smelling of honey and resin. The sky's deep blue. How earth sings and forest breathes! Scales stir from golden trunks. As though they'd been sundered from the sun. From the heat, everything around wishes to shatter joyfully, like this chip, with a dancing sound.

On a stump, the dragonfly unbends its glass wings in an onrush of sun; they shimmer as the heat flows along them.

A hunter of harmonies and thoughts has stretched out, face down, and he's basking. The dragonfly-jewel-princess rocked above his shoulders, then sat gracefully below his back—taking that part for a hillock. It shines like a precious ruby on his trousers. He doesn't even suspect this adornment—or the little tuft at his brow either. Together these give him a foolish and kindly appearance. The dragonfly glints ruby-like on his tattered trousers; while before his wide—as if enchanted only now—eyes... another, deep blue, rises and falls, rises rocking on the honied surges of summer.

*
    *   *

Something in my breast is pleading so nicely today.

My soul responds to the resinous day.

My soul seeks something great, something select, some depth, some endless treasurehouse, something possible.

Right here it's still dry and needly beneath my feet; below is the green little bank of a mysterious ditch, and the sacred green urns of the ferns perform a rite... The soul is pleading in my breast.

Then the pines' soul comes to me with resinous, fluid unrest and speaks these mysterious words:

"You know, you're the only one!

Know that you're ours, remember! The Herald Spirits sent you here. For us. And it's we who've filled you.

Know as well that here, in our name and that of nature —left wounded and defenseless by man—you must..."

At that moment they call me to dinner.

—Coming! Coming right away!..

How tiresome!..

*
* *

Long live glorious galoshes! Whoever finds a pair of galoshes (missing their miserable human legs) in the forest of
the Baltic seacoast—let him know that they're my galoshes.
They were too proud, too great to stay on my feet. Lofty
ones! Fortunate is he whom they call friend, he on whose
feet they agree to wend. They always despised me.

Rainl t, rainlet, ring out on the roofs of the glorious
song of self-reliant galoshes!.. They were so nobly autono-
mous, so salon-trained that they almost never remained in
the entry... Oh no! And I'd notice that only when, quite
deservingly, they'd managed to attract the attention of everyone seated in some drawing room.

I'm not envious—but they always got more attention
than I. I couldn't bear the rivalry.

And now... alone, proud, somewhat sad—they're free.
O, galoshes, galoshes, glorious galoshes of the north!

Oh you! your shirt's sticking out over your belt!

Looks like you've got room for twenty pounds of flour to be dumped inside it.

Spread your fingers like rakes, eh? Oh, you shilly-shally.

What are you staring at—with your mouth open too!

Can you manage a rowboat?

No.

A horse?

No.

Can you fight?

No, really... leave me alone!

What do you do all day then, you big dummy?

C'mon, lay off... that's enough...

Oh, I'd beat the stuffing out of you, but why bother... and besides, you're a king—the sky and earth are yours, personally...

Ah, the heck with you!... you'll stand there gaping until Christmas. You know what, I'll belt you one, purely out of compassion or else you—a king—will go on standing like that until Christmas.

Bleached by salt water and sun, pine cones on the deserted sand take on a sky-blue color.

Each cone contains a crystallized tempest in the unfolding of its curved fish scales. A stubborn wind—crystals of a northern mood. They were gathered in a cap and brought home, along with snail shells smelling suspiciously of slime and nice little dry balls which those at home threw away since they were clearly produced by hares. And their gatherer was ridiculed because of them. Really ridiculed! Fending them off, he fought his way through the bushes... and left clumps c⸍ fine hair on twigs. He stumbled like some laughing-stock and dashed like a young giraffe. Why? You see, the little hare balls were dry and very nice. They lay in the dimpled sand as though in little nests.

There's a very solemn mystery which must be revealed to mankind.

> We, by the grace of God, dreamers—
> Issue our decision!

All poets, makers of future signs—must go barefoot while the earth is seized with summer. Our feet are still innocent and simple-hearted, inexperienced and easily enraptured. The smooth salty sand seems slightly frozen beneath bare feet, and only between toes do those now-hot, now-cold currents stir. The earth converses with naked feet. Beneath a bare foot a board will sing of heat. And only then will you know your nearness to it.

That is why it follows unfailingly for poets to go barefoot in summer.

*
* *

It's a positive disgrace to spend the whole day heating your heels in the sand!

Only apostates of their faith, betrayers of their homeland are capable of that—those who don't celebrate its beauty or defend that beauty with the power of the word...

> O, laziness, mighty laziness!
> My dreamy laziness!

How broad everyone's breast seems today! From the little dune comes a smell of salty morning. It's like swallowing chill waves.

Taking light timid steps some barefooted, fair-legged vacationing boys passed; their soles weren't used to it yet, and they often pricked them on pine needles.

The pines are lullabying... sunny shadows tenderly dissolve into the milk of the air.

Tender, curly white creatures have sailed from the south and melted into the upper air's blue beverage.

Wind, tickle me softly behind the ear!.. No, not that way! No one's asking you to tickle my nose! And airy eccentric, I don't need you to tell me that my nose is a little long... What?.. It isn't true! It wasn't I who knocked over my aunt's plant stand and brushed the vase of flowers off the table! I'm always agile, I'm slender... I was born to dance delightfully—I'm a prince! Sand, tickle my left ankle... that's the way!..

My lovely cloud... my lovely caressing cloud... my little white calf of the sky... dreamy with a dream of sky...

S. Šypo.

THE SUN AT LAST

The young German tutor is standing in the garden. His back's a little lonely, but just now the sun's warmed it. His arms dangle and his legs too. When walking, he keeps his mouth slightly open—for the sake of balance—and his appearance is a bit crazy. But on the other hand he's glorious when he gives a contented little roar in a bass voice recently received as a gift from mother nature. Not yet able to manage a man's voice, he sometimes over-roars and then glances guiltily at the house.

The caressing sun warms him.

Sometimes even a very modest young man thinks: "How nice I am!" and wants to stroke under his chin.

It's impossible on a kind sunny day not to love one's own cheeks or round chin.

Then he becomes embarrassed.

Another young man is moving his jaws and ears in an angry, business-like manner... chewing bread? No, a whole big bar of chocolate. It looks absurd, and you can't help loving him for it.

Joyful hour in the forest!

In the forest, bearberry blooms!.. small rosy flowers.
All the earth, the mounds of moss are a mass of almond foam!

Earth's immersed in rosy foam!

Ah, blissful air, joyful hour!—
In the forest, bearberry blooms with fragile flowers!!!

CHILDREN OF THE SUN

Some the sun warms so gently, so richly that it's all the same to them—to go right or left, to lead their society into a swamp or out by some opportune path—as long as the sun shines, loving them.

They lose their way, plunk their feet into puddles, forget the quaking of the treacherous forest swamp. It seems too nice everywhere for them to notice the road.

Instead of envying them, others laugh at them and get terribly angry.

But the sun keeps caressing, caressing the dear scatterbrain while he crawls along, brushing against everything, losing his galoshes or sneakers, his pocket inside-out like a donkey's ear... and he hums to himself from the joy of dreaming amid mounting general indignation.

. . . .

Since one of the members of the colony lost his books in the forest, while *We* gathered them up—

We're giving him notice—we've done with doing it.

"In the future, don't forget them!"

May your fame resound, balconies of vacant dachas, sand pits, slopes, little barns!

There, summer-long, they collected to confer, there they proclaimed marvelous mottos of art! There were the clumbs of dreamers, when some sat, their legs shoved under them, on little steps; and the bravest, half-witted one with enchanted blue eyes, waving his hand in measure, declaimed in a consumptive's muffled bass, while in the descending dusk, white beans showed forth and summer shirt sleeves seemed wings, and a few bentwood chairs from the dacha furnishings listened with open mouths as they faced his verses.

O, beauty, in whose name they sit and meekly cough in their unheated garrets!..

A lovely star shone through the lattice of the balcony.

Вдохновенье!

Е. Бурс.

Your violin's gone slightly mad. It's day, day, day, and we believe in spirits! With fair hair and a kindly face, a spirit is strolling in the sky, between the birches. Some sky-blue has adhered to his footsteps. How happy you and I are! You believe that settling down as a family man, one can again be God; that already high-ranking, one can reform, can recognize how Mozart mastered the sky-blue of the birch—and that tomorrow is the goal of today.

We rocked in a hammock and daydreamed about the soul's immortality, young pines stood sunflooded.

Hinges creaked.

We almost considered ourselves spirits.

The swing swept up. Eternal youth—you know, it is attainable!

*

*   *

—Why don't you want to?

—Why don't I want to?! Because they get published and get their things accepted there through connections; the cowards bootlick in order to gain entry there, and then block the doorways and push the young aside and refuse to let them enter because they're talented—they leave them in the darkness....

—We're well-known—you're not! People won't know a thing about you—they follow those we write about. What entitles you to want the light?

—I'm talented!

—What's that to us?

—I thirst for light!

—How does that concern us?

—I'm a man!

—Our light doesn't have to satisfy everyone.

—I want to serve people!

—That's another matter—forget your thirst and your fantasies.

*

* *

Why don't you get going on something? Or are you observing St. Indolent's Day today?

Now leave "indolence" alone. Each month has only five St. Indolent's days:

(1) When I don't feel like it. (2) When I can't get started. (3) When I plan to start tomorrow. (4) When I'm all set to start work, but it's time to rest. (5) When I couldn't care less about anything.

The dacha's awnings flap like sails. They're filled with a salt-sea smell.

—Hey! Don't sleep! Cut it out! Well, what about the proof-sheets?

—Why don't you get lost? I'm dreaming, and anyway...

—That's enough! Are we putting the magazine together or not? If it isn't ready by the eleventh, I'll give you a good drubbing with my cane. I mean it. I'm leaving.

—Wait, have you heard? Wait a minute—a fir crashed across the ravine, nearly crushed our whole brook.

—So what else is new?

—God knows what's happening at sea... it's seething every which way.

—Well, either the proof-sheets, or...

—Oh why don't you just go to hell!!

*

*   *

The sky is radiantly pale. In the bright feathers of clouds as they spread—there's a sign of their span, a sign of soaring, and the firs' crosses cut like masts into all that.

In pine boughs—everywhere—thousands of sleepy rhythms drowse.

Pines give forth so much silence that it devours sound. Days, golden trunks, thoughts, people are immersed like fish, in bright June.

I pray to the quiet protectors, with their wings wide and tender, like a vast sea and a quiet dune.

"My songs will make people better," he thinks. And he goes lightly along the walkway, and glances around. "I hope they'll become sincere, honest, good—and braver—" here he smiles, a bit embarrassed—you see he himself isn't always brave.

"Why will they be better from my songs? Is it because this shapely little pine will be in my songs? Pink transparent heather, so pure in its pink that no one can help loving it? If you really love some slender treetop, can you then decieve someone?

No, never!

Will I write these songs or not? Is this fate mine or not?"

Softly, softly, sweetly it's breathed about: "Mine? mine?" He prays. . . "but is this road mine? Suppose it isn't mine? . ."

Softly, softly, sweetly the heart suffers. It wants the pangs of conscience—wants to suffer—and it can't: there's so much time ahead for reforming.

Ahead, one after another, young treetops—pure and slender—measure the sky.

Just looking at them, how can you help being honest?

How can you feel anyting except joyful expectation?

In some sly way he wants to languish, to be a sinner, to repent. . . wants to reform.

Will people love my songs? Will they love my pine?

Like a light slender cross, its tip rushes into the care-free gentle sky.

Timid summer-vactioners pass right by him and in their fear, they put on a harsh and scornful air. While he steps aside in confusion, and jumps from the walkway.

Е. Гуро.

*
* *

On the horizon, a luminescent little piece of an un-attainably joyous land looked out from birches heavy with rain—a path was shown, leading there. But it was a laughable path, and one believed in unattainable joy.

*
* *

A shy young man loved flowers. They thrust up from the earth in innocent astonishment, and the face of each was irreplaceable; and it would have been terribly sad and cruel to deceive one of the trusting... the joy of each little white star, each frail little cup, each exposed heart.

But the large and gentle hands knew how to touch what was new to them with such delicacy of compassion and foresight, that in this kingdom of defenselessness no one feared the soft approaching footsteps of this large, incomprehensible creature.

Because there's a perfectly straight road into the sky... above the high, straining branches and the roof's sloping. Where boughs are like birds, like swords, crosses, and portents.

It was a dawdling day—milk-soft and still. He'd already noticed before that the trunks of young pines are music strings. Their boughs... uplifted.

The young pinewood stands like a quiet slender fire. "Star, my star... no that's not the word... Ah you, my quiet doe"..... Thus he named not some girl, but his life. Because it was very meek. He hadn't loved yet.

There was no wind in the high-up places... He stood a long long while... He didn't promise anything to those strings. But, something was pronounced before them, on his behalf... he didn't hear, but he felt it.

He didn't say a word. And sighed, not knowing why he sighed. He returned quietly, dragging his feet.... And was late for dinner. They bawled him out.... He carved on the table with a pen knife, secretly. Thought awhile... Examined his middle finer.... Thought.......

That's how he was promised to life.

DREAM

Gentler than a cloud will be my love when I love,
    but I haven't yet loved;
Gentler than the smile of a cloud will be my love,
    but wait—I haven't loved yet.
Clearer than a lake will be my love,
    but I haven't yet loved.
Or is it already possible? Is it time? Time that a
rosy fog rise over reeds by the lake, and not lift? I'll glance
from sandbar to sandbar witha crane's sharp sight, catching
in the morning fairness the clearest branch of some pine.

*
  * *

You're my joy.
You're my treetop at a lakeshore.
My music string. My evening. My horizon.
My pure twig in a sky gone pale.
My evening horizon—high, high up.

Stormy petrel, rusher, rascal—
The raging wood awaits you!
It's proud crowns have risen to the clouds...
The brothers are working up a storm!
You won't hear the voice of your sorrow
When they start their rabid singing
And wave their branches in the roily sky.
Oh those brothers!
They've raised their paws in the sky;
In tumult they rumple their needles.
Stormy petrel, tender dreamer,
You catch stars
In the gaps with the fir...
With your gaze you gather lingonberry rubies
Into the seines of your tender, beautiful stupidity—
And strands of cranberry onto carpets.
With your eyes you catch stars
And let them slip back into the sky...
Spreading your toes slightly,
You let slip
The locks of hot light.

Evening. Long, thin, faintly sad strips on the horizon.
"You see, you sometimes have to go barefoot through nettles." He spoke, fell silent, and thought to himself: "Well, I guess you do then." He thought it over, biting his fingers a bit. He regretted having said it.

He was a very shy eccentric. Going off to the side, they were already laughing and mocking him. On the horizon, above the smooth sand of the dune, a gull riveted a rusty nut.[1] The pines of the Kalevalla seashore waved and sailed away. There was no splash. An evening eye, brimming with silence, rested by the shore.

> Dreaming land,
> nothern strand,
> shoreless gaze—
> great and great-hearted.

There was an astonishingly bright strip in the sky. Since he'd asked for it, he really did have to go barefoot through nettles for it. That's why she left him.

It seemed absurd and shameful to her when his bare foot got stung and flinched involuntarily, awkwardly.[2] And he was so simple-hearted that he bravely plowed barefoot through the nettles. But sometimes his foot twitched absurdly from the pain. That's just what they couldn't forgive him.

Poor lovely miss—she didn't know how to fly!..

1. The reference is presumably to a gull's cry. [Trans.]
2. This passage is similar to one in Guro's "An Autumnal Dream" *(Osennii son)*, Act II, in which a "Jolly Miss" mocks Wilhelm. [Trans.]

*

* *

A road lay off to the side.
You couldn't travel it.
　　Oh no!
And because of that, it was very beautiful!
　　Yes, just because of that.
A road caressed the earth—
Clung to it so it took your heart away.
　　We came to love that road...
　　Grass had overgrown it.
Fate, fate, my little fate!
My quiet fate, my quiet one.
What do you hold for me, or I for you?
　　You who have tormented me!

This ache, when the heart bursts into space—with love for tree, evening, sky, bush. And loves because it cannot, cannot deny love.

*
* *

What do we know about beauty?.. We consider hunchbacks unbeautiful, but in our crudeness we've simply overlooked their beautiful hour. And for want of warmth, their beauty went away.

Thus we ourselves create forgotten beauty, and then it pursues us, stings us and demands the warmth it was denied, the light it was driven from—bereft of that light, it simply went away, while we prayed in awe before the repulsive, haughty face of Juno.

Why are hunchbacks considered unbeautiful?—after all, they have hours of beauty, while Juno has only her drooping, malicious, sensual lips and the moments of her sharp, hen-like greedy eyes. But they've convinced us that a straight nose and arched eyebrows are beauty, absolute beauty.

There's a delicate smell of algae, algae. The sea loves everyone. God's will gives off its deep warmth. God, having formed this dune, God, Protector, help me—I'm not cunning. True God of this grey dune, you care for your little grey birds on the sand. I'm not cunning, but I have many enemies. I'm something of a bird, help me.

Don't you know that from a single dream of yours, storms are born? That from a single pure dream sometimes storms are born?!..

NIGHT

It thawed at night. The sky stood wide open. A light rain fell. No, it was a drizzling fog. Leaf-buds hung near streetlights, shimmering on almost imperceptible bare twigs. Spring was blossoming forth. The soul could barely believe it and stood completely naked and kindly, and believed deeply in everything. Anyone might have wounded it, if it hadn't been sheltered by the mystery of night. Spring was in the soul. Mist rose, there was a smell of earth, a light rain fell.

—Do you love sand?

—I love it, it's soft.

—Do you love pines?

—I love them—if you press a cheek against their sunny side, they're warm.

—And do you love that horse?

—I love her. She has nice nostrils.

—Do you love the sea?

—Yes. I've noticed that on quiet days it loves me.

—Do you love the earth?

—How can you ask, after all, she's my mother!

.   .   .   .

When I stare at the starry sky, I think: "Are the spirits of other stars as kind as earth is kind?"

And I feel like crying from compassion for her. They're always taking something from her.

I want to protect her.

I will protect her!

*
*   *

Like a flag or a pennant rushing atilt into the deep-blue sky, you rushed to meet the wind, my springtime.

I know you believe in me. You believe that when I sit in the forest all day, absurdly lost in the comtemplation of some mound, and apparently doing nothing, that there's more to it that that, that it's not all in vain. That when I speak of failures, it's before the sincerest efforts.

You believe in me. You believe in me so you're able to wait for my sake. You believe in me when I don't believe in myself and when I believe in myself as in God! You're never angry with me because of that! And people usually get angry because of that.

You believe. God grant you a kindred wind and kindred earth. The shaggy, sharp-tipped treetops sway over this our kindred earth. On this our kindred earth, wooded distances unfold endlessly and the sharp treetops dash, like daredevils, into the sky—they sway in the wind over potato fields.

On this our kindred earth there are different dawns and a special wind.

TOGETHER

—You've got to have a pure, sincere soul to be a knight.
—What are you doing then to improve yourself?
—I go in the morning to a young pine and measure my present feeling of purity against its height, but it's almost cruel...

—And you told me this! I can see now what your're like...

Do you believe in me?
—I believe in you.
What if everyone turns against me?
—Well yes, how funny you are! I believe in you.
If all my actions come to disgrace me?
—I do believe in you!
A swallow flies off, off into the sky and whirls with joy. It's bleak, grey, and quiet at the dune.
A little snipe clings to the sand.

ADAGIO

Two pines on the shore of the dune form a chalice. The sides of the divine golden chalice are formed by the diverging trunks. Its base is where the two trees rise together. The upper areas curve into the clouds, like the sad curve of a seaside country. Whirlwinds are within the whispy needles.

We called that chalice the chalice of depth, of reverie and faithfulness.

STUDY OF A YOUNG PINE GROVE BY THE SEASHORE

An overcast lilac sky—it's turning evening. How slender they are!

I love you because you have wings—wings still covered with the down of first youth. A golden ringing delicate down, while your wings, your wings, are by the sea.

The sea is deep blue and distant—a strip to which daring flies, and farther off, it merges with blue—and I don't know whether dream or blueness lies farther.

And I don't need to know—what difference does it make?! The down of the young winged heroes is ringing—and their shapeliness is sometimes misshapen and unexpected as early growth.

And they've dashed upward to glory, to their native land where the clouds are lost in thought... And I don't need to know anything else about you. I believe in you—you call me with voices of valor—they burn me like the flame of purity, and up above, the clouds over me are lost in thought.

I'm going, and that's all I need to know!

Did you ever ask yourself why you go in the morning to the edge of the forest—and stand there and wait? That place of pure brown earth, littered with big pine needles. Why do you need that?.. When at the same time it torments you!..

It's cold in your soul then. Why is it also pleasant?

"It" will be revealed this very instant, right here in the silence. Then I will bear it in my heart, fearing to say a word about it. What was always awaited in those harsh early silences will be revealed!

What was awaited, what has never yet been, but which is near, which draws painfully near and when you already love it to the point of tears—does not come. And that alone is worth an act of heroism.

That's why you go the the area of bare, tall, lonely trunks—and gaze.

Why you go to the pure, untouched earth of the forest and wait.....

There's a green strip gleaming above the pines.

.　　.　　.　　.　　.　　.　　.　　.　　.　　.　　.　　.　　.　　.　　.

And they betrayed him... He said, "Oh well, there are others somewhere. After all there's me and I'm faithful."

And he placed his sky-blue hope in his palms and shifted it up higher. Caressing it, he tossed it up gently. It flew above the treetops and settled higher up. Where an inaccessible silver-green strip lay.

And where purity and faithfulness were, and no one ever hurt it again.

Summer goes by with firm, quiet steps. Blue waterfalls have spilled amid trees. Brimful of blueness, a smooth stream pours from the sky.

Bright sunspecks fall in cascades from the birches. Sunspecks, sunspecks... like a silver sound.

A shone-through forest shines. Somewhere time passes. The sun flows round each trunk. From the shining of numberless grassblades, the forest is flooded with some special, water-like substance—it's an underwater world. And somewhere far off, time goes by. A frail branch of lingonberry or heather has bent oddly and glows strangely—this makes everything radiant and magical.

There's no time, as such.

I noticed that a tiny lingonberry plant with stiff leaves (like the wings of a little green beetle) lives in the pinewood at the foot of some giant's columns. And it belongs here.

If your head's fairhaired or grey, now the light shines on it also. If you glance aside, into that darkness there's a feeling of warm blessedness.

They you'll become aware of something more ancient, more ancient, but what, you yourself don't know.

They you see that an ordinary bluebell on a crooked stem has bent round and is staring at you. And a dark cleft in the bark of a birch, below which the pale-navy bluebell stands, also is staring at you...

Then somewhere in your being you become partly bluebell, and it partly you. Now it doesn't occur to you to pluck it or tread on it with indifference. Then since you've become acquainted with one, other beings will respond.

From everywhere now, the tiny sharp tails, little mounds of moss, leaves, dry twigs, spots on tree trunks are staring at you.

Then you don't feel like leaving the forest.

.   .   .   .

*
*   *

When the wind's so warm,
I feel like grabbing a little handful—
wind, my little wind.....

*

*   *

She was depressed all day because her shoe was untied. She didn't dare stop and tie it, and went by everyone with her shoe untied. Depressed too because she'd replied seriously to a joke—when she should have laughed. And she didn't realize—oh, how stupid it was, unbearably awkward and stupid.

Everything told me something big lay ahead. And then I seemed to hear big footsteps in life. On a hilltop my head started to spin.

Stomp, stomp, who's coming through the dark garden?

Is it my fate? Is it my future? (But I realize I'm speaking too boldly and I try to be sly.) I really don't deserve anything; I'm untalented, untalented, but on the other hand, I'm meek, I'm very meek, and I'd be happy to go on living this way, a little at a time... Hear it? It's coming!

Is it my fate? My future?

And at evening tea I hunch over my cup so I won't be noticed. And the cup seems incredibly blue, impossibly deep blue.

At such times I seemed to hear big footsteps and perhaps... Perhaps something in life loved me, but I grew too mean and gloomy. And then there were betrayals and apostasies and obesitites.

Now my heart is big and my disposition mean, very mean.

And now the brook beneath the hill sucks at my heart also, and flows toward an impossible emptiness. Little has been left, only some indifferent objects—then there's emptiness. Impossible emptiness. And really it's already impossible.

A boy ran by on a roundabout path, and drove a hoop.

. . . .

Why don't I express what makes me grow weak with delight? How can I discover my real, cherished thoughts? So I won't compose what's alien and accidental. After all, something springlike can get through to me. A boy ran by (a little striped shirt on his back), and I caught the fleeting, divine scrape of the hoop and the sandy path.

Deep within the forest, ferns—like delicate snakes— grew toward water and made the black earth green. A new bucket (with its fresh pink wood) grew wet. Above the bucket, in a transparent willow a bird sang—as though rinsing its throat with the tender sky.

And in spring, the souls of trees are so inaccessibly pure that the people below seem anguished, unable to bear themselves.

Lord, if only I wouldn't always busy myself with alien things—scattering someone else's beautiful words, and with tears of enthusiasm in my eyes! It's really suicide.

A pine bucket. A deep blue snowdrop, shyly wilted. It's blueness is painful. Lord, deliver me from someone else's beauty. Deep within, I really am sincere and fervent. Why will this—blue and tender in the grass—fade, uncared for? Why will its unbearably spring-like beauty fade without leaving a trace, the victim of time and someone's platitude— while I remain guilty, and with the words of someone else's beauty on my lips. As though the sky, and the greenery's light hadn't touched me.

After all, this is the murder of your earthly green happiness. This is murder. Besides, the transition from violet color to rose in the petals of some tiny mossy flowers was a guarantee of life's highest mission—immeasurable sincerity and purity. And the moss, in its velvet, vaguely recalled the warm earth.

And my soul is tormented with responsibility for the departing moments.

*

*   *

Evening. Upper air is radiant. I look at a poplar's soaring trunk.

Why am I so depressed? And I don't understand—where is our depth? Why do we move away from it? And losing our depth, with it our real voice? And shall we no longer find our roads?

You, sacred poplar, boundlessly branching into the sky. Always proud, always true, always sincere. You are the sky's truth...the depth's sacrifice. Spirit of grandeur.

In the delicate crystal birches are signs of deathless life. Signs that the fragments of meetings and partings flung here, and seemingly momentary—are filled with an eternal and certain significance.

Well, so be it. Inaccessible ones, you probably know why I'm sentenced to my inability here. That's probably so.

The grassy wind bent so low it was brown and warm; it smelled of potatoes.

A long, long potato wind. A patient long-legged wind from some field.That's how I imagine my homeland.

Returning. It's warm. I'm a bit ashamed of my failures, still I feel like singing the praises of my potato field. But I don't feel like being mocked. I'm ashamed! You have to be sincere and not worry about feeling ashamed.

So I crossed the little wood. At its edge a rosy sunset shone through the thin pine branches.

The sunset! The rosy-cheeked sunset!

There are things not shameful before God, but shameful before men. Others, before God, are unbearably shameful, while before men they're even pleasant. But it's impossible to remain alone with those at the sunset edge of a pinewood.

And so you can go to the edge of a pinewood and cleanse your soul amid the tall, mast-like trunks. —Something mighty is watching him... Is he bad or good? "More likely bad," you agree softly... Is this my path? What is my calling?.... Forests will fade, but me of the future will be good and tender, will allow each thing to grow as it wishes, will restore the free life...

*
*   *

Oh you tinder warrior! Prince! Oh, you hero stuffed
with wet tow! Does it feel good to fly head over heels from a
stumbling steed? To fall from dream castles into a crowd of
mockers, and to gaze with those frightened blue eyes?

      What's all this softness!
      There's warmheartedness for you!
      There's creativity and sensitivity!
      What? You don't like this?
      How dare you be tender,
      When everything must be aimed toward systematic
                                  firmness,
      Endurance, health and strength?
      Fix his bearing!
      Don't dare hunch! Stand straight!
      Don't gawk, look respectfully!
      We're your judges, we're your justice—we're your...
      What softness.

*
*   *

*
* *

Nasturia wither on their long poles.
Peat bogs give off a sharp smell of burning.
Deep souls roam lonely.
Summer has grown overripe with the heat.
Don't touch me with your evil current...
Amid the rustles and smells of the overripe, withering
summer,
A thoughtful gaze wanders...
Quiet and questioning.
Young with angels' eternal youth, and wise—
Mournfully that gaze drinks in the coming bondage, prison,
and withering
Of its exile from the lands of summer.

Now in the pink paradise of the cleanly bathed sea, inexplicable green strips began to sparkle and swim. I felt sad from the sky's clearness and from something which couldn't be expressed—there was no explanation. The young green strips swam—aglitter—and there was no answer. And all that while the paradise of light and water stood unbearably, irrevocably before my eyes.

Why is it absolutely necessary that something within you yearn, strain, ache with ineffable happiness—and has it never had any resolution?

In a blissful dacha paradise, the window frames of a balcony are edged with a band of green glass so summer days will flow by more happily. For the same reason, the balcony turns into a light, all-wooden gallery and joins the buildings. The low, narrow, covered porch (with three steps) is pensive. From it a narrow, curving path—narrow for one and just barely, two—slowly and carefully skirts a lawn with great tall trees; and forks and turns aside where a sickly birch waits and dreams at the edge.

Behind the lawn is a little ditch hugged by a fir grove— its edges are slick from the polished needles.

If you slip on them and fall, you'll get stung on the nettles at its bottom and get scratched by some kind of thorns and sharp jutting things.

Then, set with brick, the path goes off across the ditch to a grassy place.

You could play a friendly game of cops and robbers and hide among the jasmine bushes.

At the fork, a birch points toward the hushed west.

A linden is looking at the balcony.

Only recently on the little steps sprinkled with autumn leaves, they had sat and read. With its canopy, a hollow linden has inclined its intelligent, curly head and knows that beneath it they said goodbye on the eve of their departure, and believed. And beneath the linden a notebook of verses had been forgotten as well. It got soaked—a light rain had fallen at night. The deep blue cover ran a bit. But because of that the notebook became still dearer to someone.

Then the path goes off, carefully unbending, down along the slope. Just as though throwing a friendly invisible arm across your shoulders, and leading you along.

Down below is a pond; there's a plain wooden raft on it. Here the minutes always halt, motionless and beautiful. Someone, lost in thought, was late for supper.

The dark reflected sky of the pond is deep.

There's always another deep purple, mute country in the pond.

The surface of the wooden raft is bleached silvery by rain and sunlight, and it's possible to stand and believe there, to promise, to become involved, share solitude, to grow close and express sympathy.

But in the birch mirrored in the deep depth and in the beautiful crimson twilight country of reflections—where the dark sky is different and the clouds float into the depths transformed by the crimson twilight—there's something that can't be fathomed or retained. And it's a pity that it goes away.

Up above is a tender stand of yellow birches and their slender dream hasn't yet seen its loftiest day of knighthood. Life turned and, not having lived, became a memory. It's a pity—but then, in the mind, they've escaped time and shackles.

Now they no longer belong to anyone.

Along the edge of the hill a fence of boards, somewhat aggressively forbidding and sharp, totally shuts off the neighboring properties. The thick brick posts of the future wall are a testament to someone's possessive enmity.

But some young larches rise by the fence, so transparent that they contain yearning, a dream and courage. And someone dug a little hole through the fence, where the boards were detached from the post, and having slipped into the garden you can again go along the narrow, pensive path around the lawn to the birch at the edge, and then it leads down carefully to where the minutes halt, beautiful, beside the pond and the wooden raft.

*

* *

Some eyes were so tender in youth that after petting the first little dog they met on the street, they then asked for a moment's approval and sympathy from stern, alien, unfamiliar eyes—those of the dog's owners. After all, it seemed that for a moment something had united them. Their feeling of tenderness had met in the dog! The feeling of tenderness common to all men. But not meeting encouragement from the stern owners of the nice, intelligent dogs, they grew confused and lowered their gaze to the indifferent stones of the pavement.

And then years passed. And they had to learn to live among those stern street acquaintances... the familiar and unfamiliar owners of dogs.

—And that's all?

—That's all!

—So they learned how?

—No, of course they didn't. That's why that's all.

E. Гуро.

*
* *

They were an enchanting married couple. With a cosy nest... They came across him on a cold deserted road. And they took in the lonely, abandoned child.

He was shown kindness, and became trusting. He learned to smile and look merrily into people's eyes. He began to blurt out his fantasies to them—they called him a little boy and stroked his hair. And once again he began to confide something precious, which, generally, he didn't dare speak about—and something else about what makes people poets—friendless child, he'd found a homeland and a home. From his delight with them, morning burst forth in him. Then it stung them: here was something which might make their sober, orderly life apper a bit base.

He began to get in the way and be annoying—a grown-up, ill-mannered boy whom they'd bound to themselves in an access of superfluous sociability and philanthropy. "Be quiet!.. You're already going too far, young man!"... But he couldn't be quiet, the sun was already blazing in him. He even allowed himself to argue with their guests... Then they threw him out—that is, they showed him rather plainly that he was superfluous there. Immediately all his stars went out, and his wings broke. He himself even understood that it was impossible to stay—he left quietly. They had only let him leave by himself... When his stooped shoulders were disappearing behind the gate into the gathering darkness, they looked at one another. "Really it's a pity that just now it's such a cold night! Why couldn't he have waited till morning." She thought a bit, in irritation. Her spouse made his way home with simply bouyant little steps, and then they forgot about it. They lit their enchanting lamp. They were happy together. Past their house went the night and a long road.

Still, life's beauty was for him, and not for them. And the birches rustled for him, and not for them.

There was still another one.

He cried out like a young jackdaw, trying to get them to let him in where it was bright.

—Let me in. It's beautiful where you are.

—May I ask just who or what you are?

—I'm...

—Why do you think there's a place for you where it's beautiful? We created the beautiful and bright. We're its priests—and our chosen ones.

But You?

—You see, I really... I love art passionately, and life's so unbearably grey and boring without it.

—Well, so what?..

—But I'm ready to give my life for it—that's how I love it.

—Well, what's that have to do with us?

And they closed the door.

*

*   *

We gathered around a lamp in the living room.

The evening clung and seemed to tremble slightly, behind the window panes.

From love, for whom?

There was a thin, white, youthful lattice around the panes. They were clean, thin and painted white. That gave them an air of extreme youth.

We simply couldn't shake off the idea that someone was going to come that evening.

We had to call him and let him in.

To open to him the doors of the heart.

*

*   *

At last they took in the poet, creator of worlds.[1] Those who understood him, of course, and didn't despise his wild hair or his huge, fierce, untamed blue eyes. The artists left in the morning, and they found him at evening, pale. He trembled all over and scowled. He'd forgotten to eat, or else couldn't find anything all day, with his fierce eyes and wood-goblin hair. They learned of this by accident, and roared with laughter: "He hasn't eaten! Forgot to eat! Good show! He's trembling like a chicken—all bent over, with his stomach sucked in."

Some canned food turned up among the palettes. They bought some sausages from the back entrance of a shop.

It was one in the morning. They bought them and returned. And presto—they were fast asleep.

Dawn played tricks. Water froze in a cup. Everyone slept well. Only the poet got cold. Because one blanket was bunched up on his shoulders and the other on his heels, while his back luxuriated in the air. And the Norns prophesied to him: "You shall not be warm, poet—though you should have two warm blankets, a swarm of acquaintances and seven aunts—you shall not be full or warm.

---

1. This is a portrait of Khlebnikov. [Trans.]

I fear for you. You're too much like some fluffy straw-berry shoot, crawling out from the earth. And it's not for nothing that you kiss kittens between their ears.

I fear people will offend you.

Perhaps a little devil in a mask will come to you and say:

It's all nonsense except for the sound of a hurdy-gurdy in the courtyard...

How willingly you'll believe him...

While cars will flow along the boulevard.

And the enraged red brick buildings of the factories will go thumptata thumptata thump.

For the time being the city hides little fellows like you in pockets of the quiet, overgrown yards at its out-skirts—like thousands of other trifles, but later, later...

*

* *

They mistreated a boy's mother. He wanted to fight back, but could only counter them with silence and slip away becasue this was a big, rough, powerful enemy.

They prevented him from going to school to study: "Grow up to be a dummy!" He didn't say anything to his mother and silently hid his books.

They wanted to take his lakes from him, his lovely sky-blue lakes. He resolved to lower his white eyelashes and keep silent—that was his only defense, there was no other. He grew sullen.

"See what a little snake we've brought up! We were right to punish him; after all, he hates all of us."

He had to listen to everything in silence, mechanically twirling the handle of his basket in his hands. He was a pale northern boy. The pure sky and sea entered the broad, stubborn span between his eyes. The broad, sky-blue gaze of the sea.

He could have been cunning, but his mother had taught him to go to the Lutheran church and be honest. He loved the unbridled rocking of her treetops, her church and little cart and the scarf wound around her neck in the July heat and her song, her song.

All that was his mother: They took away his wooden toys—he kept silent. And because he didn't love them—though in silence—they took away his freedom.

FOREST THOUGHTS

I'm already thirty-four, but I fled from my own guests. What a wonderful feeling—to escape by fleeing! I had to lie with my face against the moss and old fir cones so they wouldn't notice from the edge of the forest. The forest floor is spread with moss and slender twigs. Everything in the forest is clothed in its own special forest radiance. In the forest, with every second you're more foresty. Everything foresty is very exacting—very "Don't touch me." And hides far from the outsider's reach. Bright orange scales fallen from a dark fir, grey-haired twigs sacred with rain—these the enemy never saw, never touched... No one ever disturbed their tender radiant membrane of air. Demanding, forbidding, proud forest things: pine needles—rust-colored, shining... old ones fallen from above. Some purple object. You could miss seeing all this. When at last, almost in pain, you tear yourself away from the forest and separate your soul from all this—like a puppy from its food—and go to entertain your guests: it's just like when, as a child, you went to do homework. The pain of losing what's near and dear. Probably then too there was just the same irreparable, intolerable loss.

Thoughts flow easily here, of themselves. Yesterday lots of foresty fir needles fell in my bath water. The forest was at the window.

I was thinking in the bathtub. I know a little girl the color of light straw, with transparent, almost cloud-like flesh. Her life is one of my dreams. She was brought up with tender, tender care; she knows tht she's a little lamb of the sky, a god to her mother and the servants. A servant girl was washing me and telling me about her—she loved her— "Our Tanya's always making mischief in the bathtub. Now and then the mistress deliberately tells me, 'Bring some sand to wash Tanya with!' 'No, don't you dare!' she says, 'What's this sand business! Be more careful—after all Sasha, I'm so delicate all over. Delicate legs, such a delicate little back!' And she gives them names—one leg's "Masha" and the other's "Glafira." Masha's smart, while Glafira's a mischief-maker. She starts kicking with her Glafira and splashes us all. And everyone's always tousling her and caressing her. And there was another girl. This other one no one ever caressed, and she didn't know she had a body and that it could be admired. Brusquely, they always made her hurry to get dressed after her bath: a body was just an inconvenient thing you had to hide. Once while drying the girl off after her bath, a new servant girl suddenly burst into loud, lively laughter and grabbed the girl's stomach where there was a funny dappled mole, like a beauty mark. Though she didn't know why herself, the girl became terribly offended and stamped her feet: "How dare you! How dare you! How could you! How dare you!" She shook all over with helpless, incomprehensible hurt and despair. She frightened the servant girl and hurt her feelings. She grew a little older. She was impermissably brusque, and they wanted to whip her for some monstrous crime "against etiquette." But hardly had her mother lifted her hand toward her, when the girl went into hysterics, gave a piercing scream and tore her mother's dress. They managed to pull her away only after her mother threw down the whip. Everyone must have thought she screamed from fear of pain, naturally no one ever guessed that she screamed that way from the panicky, deathly fear that they'd offend her by touching her.

Do those who create laws generally know that those laws do not punish equally?—that what's deathly cold to one, to another.... But they've sentenced both equally. Or could it be that to lawmakers, and to parents, it makes no difference?

But it's sad that this ability to take offense, this inviolability can be lost. I love both girls deeply—they are both talented and proud—but I bitterly envy one of them. You've go to protect the soul like a butterfly. Everyone understands that if you want to keep a butterfly alive, you can't rub it with your fingers.

That's how they rub what's most important from us.

And sometimes it happens the opposite way: someone comes up, and not asking whether you want it or not, teaches some dirty words, sings some ditty in your ear—and then you find the forest's no longer as foresty, the tiny flowers' forest candles aren't as sacred and magical, and there's less happiness. And you can't do anything at all to not know (as once, in your own special way, you didn't know) and you keep biting your hands.

I envy one of these girls.

THE LITTLE DONKEY

A little donkey is running along—reins flung onto its neck. A prince sits on it—bearing Spring in his eyes.

He sits sideways, legs together in royal dignity.

He's a prince, and there's no need for him to lead.

I don't know how this ended. Perhaps the donkey stumbled, the prince flew into the mud—and when he got up (all spattered and embarrassed) and saw his basket wrecked and his lovely plants scattered about, he felt terrible shame before those who marched by, full of dignity and in spotless clothes.

I'm not interested in knowing. All I need to know is this:

A little donkey ran along, and no one led it—a prince sat on it, bearing Spring in his eyes.

SPRING

A passerby went up to a lattice gleaming with greenery. He resembled the noble of La Mancha—tall, ungainly, with a brow and hands that expressed tenderness. But the north gave him light colored hair and eyes. Wearing a warm jersey.

Stopped. Placed his hand on the lattice. Gazed, couldn't tear his gaze from that greenery. Soiled his palm with dust. Rubbed it on his trousers. Tore himself away from there. Went his way.

I'm daydreaming: Suppose on just such an evening an ungainly passerby would come to my gate, and immediately, without torment, I'd read in his kind eyes that he felt good here. Nothing more. I think I'll find out in advance all sorts of ways to be nice to the lonely. I'll find out if somewhere there's someone with a tender spring brow." And I'll send him a lilac-striped scarf of tender wool, or one of white lambswool. And I'll rejoice that my tender scarf caresses his neck.

Thus the wet wind breathed of something unrealizable, springlike; and the soul became impatient.

*

* *

Tender threads of constellations make their way amid hummocks. Constellations of delicate, weak white stars. They rejoice. It's cold. Windy.

They return, discussing their exploits, life. The white constellations serve as someone's guiding thread.

—Nanny, if a kittycat marries, will it have babies?

—Uh-huh.

—The babies will grow up, but the kittycat?..

—Will grow old.

—Nanny, will the kitty die? How sad!

—The kitty will die, but it's soul will remain.

—And if the kitty was a saint? Will the kitty be an angel?

—It'll have a little halo behind its ears, a nice, bright little halo.

—It'll fly like a birdie!

—A flying kitty.

—Birdies will be scared, but it won't touch them.

—It doesn't need to anymore!

—Nanny, but do kittycats have souls?

—Are you every going to sleep, you brat?! You're going to get it!

*

*   *

I want to depict the head of a white mushroom to look wise and pure, the way it came out of the earth, having seized for itself a part of the planetary strength. To depict the walls and roof of a Finnish villa the way they appeared from the wooded hill, washed with distance and level with the clouds.

A cloud above the hill, the way it became after swimming across the bright sphere of sky.

The brows of beasts, lit by a tiny white star—as the living Goodness of breathing made them.

And my son as he began to resemble a willow with his tall bending trunk, with the little lock overhanging his brow—and a birch. And with his bright eyes—a young larch, thrusting its tip into the sky.

Only he's kinder than a willow—wearing tenderness instead of bark—and brighter than a larch. He laughs at himself. His touch blesses things.

*

*   *

I touch life with warm words, because how else can one touch something wounded? It seems to me that it's so cold, so cold for all creatures.

You see, I have no children—perhaps that's why I love all that lives so unbearably.

It sometimes seems that I'm a mother to all things.

Go far, far away my darling, my darling.

I've tortured you, I've taken your meek graceful life from you. Don't forgive me...

Ships, ships, ships far away, my darling!

Dying, she said, "You'll return! It would be better for you to depart forever for your little innocent tower in the far-away deepblue, far beyond the skyblue lands."

Oh, you'll return!.

.   .   .   .

I want him to love me more than his life, and my caress—more than the sun.

I want his soul to burst with tenderness.

But I also want him to answer my affection with the reserve of childish superiority.

"I don't have time, mommy—my train leaves in half an hour." And he'd jump into his carriage.

"I don't have time, my ships have sailed far off," the young Viking said to his bride, "and the gulls are already flapping after my ships."

And without kissing her, off he went.

And meanwhile, in the forest, the bearberry's almond snow fell, and the forest seemed in wedding attire.

I want him often to forget to say hello and goodbye.

I'm lying in bed. I'm ill. I'm waiting for him impatiently—for him to sit by me a little while.

Do I have long to live? I'm growing weak rapidly.

"Mama, imagine. I'm going away to Spitzbergen. I think I'll write my long poem better there than at our meek lakes!"

"Go! If I die before you return, madman, write in that daring poem about your mother—your mother."

That's how I dream of him.

Head lowered to my shoulder, I stood in a bright sandy thicket, feeling like a little horse with wind-swept forelock and meek, flattened tail, and glanced through the silver of the hair shining in my eyes. And because the fluff of the tall willow herbs' glassy seeds was scattering, and the needles of already faded pines were gold amid the moss—these so merged in me that I heard the resurrection of souls and the shining harbor of joy found at last, and the deep honey-dream of a youthtime of possibility and yet unheard-of creations.

And I heard the moments as living things, and the soul of their linkings, heard that there'll be a Resurrection of each tiny flake of beauty—neverending, neversetting, inextinguishable. Like the heather's rosy flowerlets. An inextinguishable harbor.

I stood like a little horse with flaxen forelock on my brow. From one side to the other in the bright clearing, glassy bits of fluff flew from tall willow herbs, shining silver.

PROMISE

Swear, you distant and near, who write on paper with your ink... on clouds with your gaze... on canvas with your paint—swear, never to betray, never once to slander the beautiful, newly formed face of your dream. Be it friendship, be it faith in people or in your songs.

A dream! You gave it life—and the dream lives—that which we've created no longer belongs to us, as we no longer belong to ourselves!

Swear this, you especially, who write on clouds with your gaze—clouds change shape—it's that easy to smear the face of yesterday's dream with unbelief.

Promise, promise! Promise this to life, promise this to me!

Promise!

In several of the sections word endings in the Russian text explicitly indicate that the speaker is male. These passages are: "You Can't Show This to Everyone" (16); "They made a fir on its roots" (30); "Long live glorious galoshes" (41); "Sundream" (45); "Why don't you want to?" (50); "Dream" (55); "Prayer on a Grey Day" (61); "Did you ever ask yourself" (66); "Everything told me something big lay ahead" (75); "June. Cloudy" (78). In all other instances, the narrator appears to be Guro herself.

Whose is this male voice, and what does Guro intend by it? Many of the short pieces that make up *The Little Camels of the Sky* describe young men, often poets and dreamers, who are awkward, simple-hearted, solitary and shy. Misunderstood, mistreated or laughed at by the world, they respond deeply to nature. The theme of Don Quixote is clearly an influence here.* Presumably Guro continued this motif in her last, never published work, *The Poor Knight*.

Guro first used the image of a camel, as well as that of Quixote, in the work that preceded *The Little Camels of the Sky, An Autumn Dream*. At one point the hero of that play, the young dreamer Wilhelm imagines how others might mock him: "Camel!.. Lanky heron!" The word for "little camel" (verbliuzhonok) is masculine in Russian. It is used as an epithet in *The Little Camels of the Sky* several times, and in each instance the subject appears to belong to that class of dreamy poetic young men.

This application of the word "little camel" provides an important clue for our understanding of the work. *The Little Camels* is a book dedicated to youth. And however the title and opening ("An Ad in the Paper") are interpreted, it was surely Guro's ready maternal sympathy for all that is vulnerable that in large measure influenced her use of gawky, docile, funny-looking camels as an emblem for the work.

I would suggest, then, that the "male" passages in the book are spoken by a "little camel," by one of those awkward, artless youths who belong to what Guro calls "the clubs of dreamers."

* See Khlebnikov's letters to Guro of April 1911 and January 12, 1913 in which he speaks of Don Quixote. In a letter (dated June 18, 1913) consoling Guro's husband on her early death, Khlebnikov says of her late works: "Here the cloak of mercy falls on the entire animal world, and people merit compassion, like the "little camels of the sky'. . . ."